Space Explorers
SUN

First Published in Great Britain in 2020 by Buttercup Publishing Ltd.
46 Syon Lane, Isleworth, Greater London, TW7 5NQ, UK

Copyright © Buttercup Publishing Ltd. 2020
All rights reserved. No part of this book may be reproduced or transmitted in any form or by any electronic or mechanical means, including information storage and retrieval systems, without permission in writing from the publisher.

Author: Andrea Kaczmarek
Illustrator: Alexandra Colombo
Series Editor: Kirsty Taylor

A Cataloguing-in-Publishing record for this book is available from the British Library.

ISBN: 978-1-912422-91-3

www.buttercuppublishing.co.uk
contact@buttercuppublishing.co.uk
Printed and bound in China

The twins, Daisy and Dan, were back at Grandpa's house for the day.

Daisy stared at a model of a sun and thought about what she had learned. She was confused about how the sun could be a star. "But it's so big and orange. It keeps us warm and the sunshine helps the plants grow," she said to herself.

Grandpa was listening, "That's right, Daisy." He sat back in his squeaky chair.

Daisy joined Dan in their spaceship, COSMODAISYDAN and began to draw. She scribbled a great big orange sun shining down on a blue and green planet. She added a little yellow moon too for fun.

"Without the sun, there would be no life on Earth." Grandpa explained. "That's why it is the most important star in the Galaxy."

"Our Milky Way Galaxy," Dan added.

"Remember, we are much closer to the Sun than we are to any other star. The Sun is much, much bigger than the Earth. In fact, it is the center of our Solar System."

Grandpa dragged out a large chalkboard. It had lots of circles and writing on it. The twins stared at it in amazement.

"Solar system …? What is a solar system, Grandpa?" Dan asked.

"Good question, Dan." Grandpa nodded. "Solar is another word for sun."

The twins groaned, "EVERYTHING in the Galaxy has two names! The moon is called Luna, we call the stars the Milky Way. Why is everything so confusing!" Daisy was getting a little bit grumpy.

Grandpa stifled a chuckle and raised his eyebrow at Daisy, she soon calmed down after that. "As I was saying ... the Sun is at the center of our Solar System and it is this that gives us life on Earth. It also gives us day and night, and the seasons, remember?"

"I remember! I remember!" Dan was jumping up and down with glee. "But we can't look at the sun through our telescope, can we Grandpa?" he asked.

"Most certainly not!" Grandpa said with a stern look on his face. "We should never look directly at the sun at all. Why do we wear sunglasses in summer?" asked Grandpa.

"To protect our eyes," Daisy nodded, "and if we go out to swim or play, we have to wear lots of sunscreen too."

Grandpa smiled and nodded in agreement.

Daisy and Dan followed Grandpa into the kitchen. He took out a large sandwich from the fridge, along with a funny green plant.

"Let's do a little experiment, science explorers." Grandpa smiled with a knowing look on his face. The twins were very excited.

"What are you going to do with that sandwich, Grandpa?" Daisy asked.
"I'm going to eat it!" he said as he shovelled it into his mouth.
Daisy laughed, "Well that's not a very good experiment, is it? What is that green plant?"

Grandpa glared at Dan as he was about to take some cheese from the fridge. Dan hesitated and took a step back.

"This is what I want you to grow my little science explorers. It is called cress, and it is delicious in a sandwich." Grandpa smiled.

They looked at each other and giggled.

Grandpa walked away and came back with two boxes.

"Take a box each. Inside you will see some cress seeds sitting on damp cotton wool. For the experiment, one of you will need to put your box in the sunlight, and the other will need to put their box somewhere dark."

The twins grabbed their boxes eagerly.

After some discussion, Dan decided to put his box of cress seeds in a dark room. He couldn't wait for them to grow!

Daisy put her box of cress seeds on a sunny windowsill. "Don't forget to water them, Dan," she said, whilst holding two watering cans.
"I'll do it for you this time."

A week had gone by and the twins were back in Grandpa's kitchen. He took out a sandwich from the fridge. "What happened with our cress and sunlight experiment?" he asked.

Daisy was very excited "My cress is green and fresh!" she said, holding her box close by. Grandpa licked his lips at the sight.

"My cress didn't grow at all," Dan said, disappointingly, "it just shrivelled and died."

"What did we learn about sunlight then, science explorers?" Grandpa smiled.
"We really need it for things to grow!" the twins exclaimed.

"I think it is time for our next big adventure! But first, let me eat my sandwich." Grandpa stuffed Daisy's cress onto the bread and took a big bite.

Back at their house, Grandpa explained their latest mission. "You know the rules science explorers, time for bed. I'll wake you up before the sun rises."

The twins yawned and did exactly as Grandpa said. They fell fast asleep, just like all good science explorers do.

As promised, Grandpa gently woke the twins before sunrise. The three of them, along with Mum, walked to a nearby hillside, with hot drinks and smiles on their faces. They couldn't wait to see the sun light up the morning sky.

"It's so beautiful, Grandpa. Look at all of the colours!" Daisy squealed with excitement and wonder. "The sun is big and yellow, but the sky is a pretty pink …" Daisy smiled up at Grandpa. "Thank you, Grandpa. This was the best mission yet!"

"Good morning, sun!" the family whispered together. What a beautiful day it was going be.

"In the infinite sky, there is a bright star, I love you Kay to the moon and back"

with love
Alexandra Colombo